Nancy Drew

AND THE CLUE CREW™

#13

Chick-napped!

By Carolyn Keene

Illustrated by Macky Pamintuan

SCHOLASTIC INC.
New York Toronto London Auckland
Sydney Mexico City New Delhi Hong Kong

CONTENTS

CHAPTER ONE

Happy Birthday!

Day 21, Mrs. Ramirez wrote on the blackboard.

She turned to the class with a big smile on her face. "Can anyone tell me what that means?"

Nancy Drew raised her hand. Mrs. Ramirez started to call on her.

But a boy named Antonio Elefano interrupted. "Uh, isn't it kind of obvious? Day Twenty-one is the day after Day Twenty." He cracked up.

Tommy Maron gaped at Antonio. "You shouldn't joke about Day Twenty-one," he said. "Day Twenty-one is the most important day ever. It's the baby chicks' due date!"

"And it's today," a girl named Gaby Small piped up. "The baby chicks will finally be born!" A bunch of students clapped and cheered.

Nancy clapped and cheered too. So did her best friends, George Fayne and Bess Marvin, who sat nearby. George and Bess were cousins, although they didn't look anything alike. They didn't act alike either. George loved sports. Bess was crazy about fashion.

For the past three weeks Nancy's class had been taking care of twelve chick eggs as part of a science project. The eggs lived inside a box called an incubator. The incubator was made of plywood and had a gooseneck lamp attached to the top of it to warm the eggs.

"Incubate" was a fancy word for helping the chick eggs to grow until they hatched. Normally the eggs would be incubated by the mother hen, who would sit on them and keep them warm until the chicks were ready to come out of their shells. The incubator was kind of a substitute for the mother hen. In fact, Nancy and her classmates had drawn a picture of a mother hen with the word "Mom" and taped it to the side of the incubator.

"Let's all gather around the incubator and see how the eggs are doing today," Mrs. Ramirez suggested. "We're going to go row by row. And remember, don't jiggle the incubator. In fact, please don't touch it at all."

Nancy was in the first row. She stood up along with the other students in her row and walked over to the incubator. She had to resist the urge to run. She was really eager to see the chick eggs!

Nancy found a good spot by the incubator and peeked inside. The twelve eggs were basking in the warm, golden glow of the lamp.

Each egg was marked with an *X* on one end and an *O* on the other. This was part of turning the eggs, which the students had done three times a day from Day 1 through Day 18. The *X*s and *O*s had helped them keep track of which eggs had been turned. Turning was something that the mother hen would have done herself if she had been incubating the eggs. It kept growing chicks from getting stuck to the insides of the eggs.

Just then, Nancy noticed something. "Mrs. Ramirez?" she said breathlessly. "Some of the eggs have tiny little cracks!"

"Oh, no, are they broken?" Bess cried out.

"No, Bess. I think it means the chicks are about to hatch," George pointed out.

Mrs. Ramirez peered inside the incubator. "George is right. Class, we finally get to see the chicks being born. Isn't that exciting?"

"Should we break the eggs so the chicks, uh, come out faster?" suggested Antonio.

"Absolutely not," Mrs. Ramirez said quickly. "No one is allowed to touch the eggs. The chicks need to break through the shells themselves."

Gaby raced up to the front of the crowd that had gathered around the incubator. She squeezed through Nancy, George, and Bess, jostling for a good view. "It will probably take a few hours for all the chicks to be born," she said to no one in particular. "Maybe all day. I know, because I'm an expert on farm animals."

"Hey, Gaby, I can't see," a girl named Maya complained.

Tommy raised his hand. "Oh, Mrs. Ramirez? I brought in a birthday cake for the chicks. It's in my locker. Do you think this is a good time to sing 'Happy Birthday'?"

Nancy, George, and Bess grinned at one another. Tommy had been the chicks' greatest fan since the beginning of the project. In the past few weeks, he had written chick poems and chick songs. He had created a "Welcome, Chicks!" poster, which was hanging on the wall next to the incubator. He had even named each of the chicks himself. Mrs. Ramirez had said that the class would have to vote on the names, though.

Tommy's number-one passion was definitely chicks!

"It's a really special birthday cake," Tommy continued. "I baked it myself. It's shaped like a baby chick, and it's got yellow icing on it. The letters are in orange icing, except that my little sister smeared the *B* on purpose so it kind of says Happy Irthday." He frowned.

"A birthday cake?" Mrs. Ramirez looked surprised. "Well, that's very nice of you, Tommy. Why don't we wait until after lunch?"

"Sure, Mrs. Ramirez," Tommy replied.

"That is the dumbest thing I've ever heard of!" someone said loudly. "Who cares about a bunch of stupid chickens, anyway?"

CHAPTER TWO

Xs and Os

Nancy gasped. So did George and Bess. Who could be saying such mean things about the baby chicks?

Then Nancy spotted Catherine Spangler standing near the back of the crowd. Catherine had her hands on her hips. Her cheeks were flushed a bright, angry red.

Mrs. Ramirez saw Catherine too. "Excuse me, Catherine, but that's not how we talk in this class," she said sternly.

"But it's not fair," said Catherine, pouting.

"What's not fair?" Mrs. Ramirez asked her.

"It's not fair that everyone's making such a big fat deal about the chicks' birthday, when really it's someone *else's* birthday and no one seems to remember *that,*" Catherine complained.

Mrs. Ramirez's eyes widened. "Oh, that's right. It's *your* birthday today, Catherine, isn't it?"

Catherine didn't say anything.

"Well, I'm very glad you reminded us," Mrs. Ramirez told Catherine. "Next time, it would be best if you let us know directly, and without using words like 'dumb' and 'stupid.'" She turned to the class. "Class, we've all been so focused on the chicks' birthday. But it's Catherine's birthday too. Why don't we gather around and sing 'Happy—'"

"Hey, there's a beak!" Gaby shouted. "The first chick is coming out of its shell!"

"Cool!" someone said.

"Let me see, let me see!" said someone else.

A bunch of kids swarmed eagerly around the incubator. "Nobody touch anything!" Mrs. Ramirez called out.

Everyone seemed to have forgotten about singing "Happy Birthday." "Hey, let's sing," said Nancy, but her voice was drowned out by the excited chatter.

Nancy gave up and peered into the incubator along with everyone else. Gaby was right; a tiny beak had emerged from one of the eggs.

A few minutes later, more pieces of the shell broke away, and a tiny yellow head popped out. And then, finally, the whole shell broke away, and the chick himself popped out, peeping and chirping. Nancy knew that it was a "he" because he was yellow. Mrs. Ramirez had explained that with this particular kind of chicken, all the boys would be yellow, and all the girls would be brown.

"It's Chirping Charlie!" Tommy announced.

"He's so cute!" George said to Nancy and Bess.

"He's the exact same color as my dress," said Bess, twirling. "We match!"

Nancy was about to say something when she noticed Catherine standing by herself, away from the crowd. She looked upset. In all the excitement over the chick, the class had forgotten about Catherine's birthday—again.

George, Bess, and I should make Catherine a super-cool birthday card during recess, Nancy told herself.

"And so by the end of the day, all twelve chicks were born!" Nancy announced to her father and Hannah Gruen at dinnertime. "Five boys and seven girls. It was really awesome!"

It was make-your-own-taco night at the Drew house. Nancy loved make-your-own-taco night. As always, Hannah had laid out platters of warm corn taco shells as well as lots of ingredients to put inside them.

Hannah had been the Drews' housekeeper for the past five years, ever since Nancy's mother died. She was way more than a housekeeper, though. She was almost like a mother to Nancy.

Mr. Drew smiled at his daughter. "That's wonderful, honey," he said. "When I was in elementary school, we did a chick project too."

"Did your class name the chicks yet?" Hannah asked Nancy.

Nancy reached for a taco shell and put it on her plate. She was going to construct the fattest, yummiest taco ever. "Well, sort of," she replied. "There's this boy named Tommy who's kind of obsessed with the chicks. He named them before they were even born. The names are Pippy Pipsqueak, Flufferina, Tinybelle,

Coco Puff, Miss Mini, Fifi Feathers, Goldy Greg, Chirping Charlie, Loud Louis, Shy Sherman, Hopping Herman, and Fred. Since there are five boys and seven girls, one of the girls ended up being named Fred." She giggled. "Tommy made a 'Welcome, Chicks!' poster, and he wrote a bunch of poems and songs for the chicks too."

Hannah pointed to Nancy's hands. "Speaking of drawing . . . you look like you've been doing a little drawing yourself," she said with a knowing grin. Nancy's hands were covered with red, yellow, and purple marker stains.

Nancy blushed. "I washed my hands before dinner, Hannah. Honest! It's just that George, Bess, and I had to make a birthday card for this girl named Catherine during recess, and the markers were super messy."

"Who's Catherine?" Mr. Drew asked. "I don't think I've met her."

Nancy explained who Catherine was. She also told her father and Hannah how upset Catherine had been about her birthday. "So we made her this card and gave it to her after recess," she finished. "I think it cheered her up."

"That was very nice of you girls," Hannah remarked.

"Absolutely," Mr. Drew agreed.

Mr. Drew then told a story about the chick project he and *his* classmates had done in third grade. While he talked, Nancy piled ingredients into her taco shell. First, shredded cheese. Then beans. Then chopped-up lettuce and tomatoes. Then sour cream. Then guacamole. Then salsa, which Hannah made herself with little pineapple bits in it, to make it sweet as well as spicy.

Nancy noticed that Hannah had put out chicken pieces, too. She started to reach for it, then stopped. Today of all days, she wasn't in the mood to eat chicken!

The next morning Nancy walked into class a few minutes early so she could check out the chicks. Other students were already there, including George and Bess. Mrs. Ramirez had moved the chicks into something called a "brooding pen." It was a very big cardboard box with a warming lamp attached to it. The bottom of the pen was lined with straw and sawdust. A sign on the side said DO NOT TOUCH THE CHICKS!

"How are the chicks?" Nancy called out to her friends as she walked over to the pen.

"They're even cuter than they were yesterday!" George replied.

Bess pointed to her outfit. "And see? Today I'm wearing brown, in honor of the girl chicks."

Nancy smiled and peered inside the pen. George was right. The chicks were even cuter than they were on Wednesday. Six of them were nestled together in a big, fluffy ball, napping. Another three were pecking at some of their special chick food, which Mrs. Ramirez had bought at the pet store. And the last three were drinking water out of their little bowl. There was lots of peeping and chirping.

Just then, Nancy noticed that something was wrong.

On the wall next to the incubator was Tommy's "Welcome, Chicks!" poster.

Someone had marked big *X*s and *O*s across the poster. It was ruined!

CHAPTER THREE

A Smelly Clue

Nancy pointed to the chick poster. "Look!"

"That's awful!" exclaimed Bess.

"Who would do a mean thing like that?" George piped up.

More kids came into the classroom. So did Mrs. Ramirez. "What's going on?" she demanded.

Nancy indicated the poster. "We all found it like this," she explained.

"Hey, who destroyed my super-duper chick poster?"

Nancy turned around. Tommy was standing there. He looked really upset.

"I worked for hours and hours and *hours* on that poster," Tommy cried out. "It was my masterpiece!"

"I'm so sorry, Tommy," Mrs. Ramirez said, putting her hand on his shoulder. Then she faced the rest of the class. "All right. I want to know right now who is responsible for this."

No one said a word.

Mrs. Ramirez sighed. "Fine. I intend to get to the bottom of this. In the meantime, I want everyone to sit down in their seats and write a one-page essay about respect. Everyone but Tommy, that is."

"You mean, like an essay about how much I respect chocolate chip cookies?" Antonio joked.

"No, Antonio. Like an essay about respecting other people's property," Mrs. Ramirez corrected him.

Nancy and her classmates worked on the essay for the next twenty minutes. Afterward, Mrs. Ramirez asked everyone to observe the chicks and write an entry about them in their chick journals. The students had been keeping the chick journals for the past three weeks, since the beginning of the chick project.

Nancy finished her journal entry quickly. Then she did something else—quietly, so she wouldn't disturb others who were still working. She checked out the area around the brooding pen and around Tommy's poster. It was possible that whoever messed up the poster had left a clue about his or her identity.

George and Bess joined Nancy. "What are you doing?" George whispered to her.

"I'm looking for clues," Nancy whispered back.

Bess grinned knowingly at her cousin. "See? I told you!"

"Have you found anything yet?" George asked Nancy.

Nancy pointed to the poster. "Well, whoever messed up the poster used a blue-green marker," she noted.

Bess squinted at the poster. "It looks more like aquamarine to me."

"No way. It's turquoise!" George disagreed.

"It's definitely aquamarine," Bess insisted.

"I know, because I have a skirt the exact same color. The salesperson at the mall said it was aquamarine. So there!" She made a face at George.

Nancy moved very close to the poster—and sniffed. "Hey, do you guys smell something?" she said suddenly.

George and Bess sniffed the poster too. "It smells kind of sweet," George said finally.

"It's candy," suggested Bess.

"I think it might be bubblegum," Nancy said.

George nodded. "Nancy, you're right. It's bubblegum!"

"So whoever messed up Tommy's poster used a blue-green or aquamarine or turquoise-colored, bubblegum-scented marker," Nancy concluded. "This is our first clue!"

"Our first clue." George smiled. "I guess this means that the Clue Crew is on the case."

The Clue Crew was Nancy, George, and Bess's special club. They collected clues and solved mysteries. In the past they had tracked down a missing ice-cream recipe, a missing City Girls doll, a missing superstar Hollywood cat, and more.

Now they were on the case to find out who had ruined Tommy's "Welcome, Chicks!" poster.

"Okay, I have an idea," George announced during art class. They were working on a special chick art project. Each of Nancy's classmates had brought in their favorite art supplies from home.

George, Bess, and Nancy were sitting at a table making chick-themed collages. "Why don't we go around the room and ask everyone if we can borrow a turquoise marker?" George continued. "That way we can see who owns one that smells like bubblegum."

"You mean an *aquamarine* marker," Bess corrected her. "I think that's a great idea."

"I agree," Nancy said. "Why don't we split up? George, you take the two tables over there." She pointed. "Bess, you take the two tables over there." She pointed again. "And I'll take the rest of the tables."

"No problem," George said. Bess gave a thumbs-up sign.

Nancy walked over to her tables. She started with Antonio. "Hi, Antonio. Do you have a blue-green marker I could borrow?" she asked him casually.

"Why, are you drawing blue-green chicks?" Antonio teased. "That's kind of weird, isn't it? Are they like mutant alien chicks from outer space or what?"

"It's for the, um, blue-green plants in the background," Nancy fibbed.

Antonio rooted through his box of markers. "Well, I don't have a blue-green marker."

"I have a blue marker and a green marker," Gaby spoke up. She was sitting next to Antonio. "As you know, it's a scientific fact that blue and green make blue-green. Maybe you could combine the two colors."

"That's okay. Thanks, anyway," said Nancy.

Nancy asked five more kids if she could borrow a blue-green marker. But no one had a marker that exact color.

A few minutes later, Nancy rejoined George and Bess at their table. "Any luck?" she asked her friends.

George shook her head. "Me, neither," Bess said. "Tommy and Maya both had aquamarine markers. But their markers didn't smell like bubblegum."

George pointed to Bess's nose and giggled. "I think you accidentally drew on your nose while you were smelling the markers. You have a big turquoise spot!"

"Oh, no!" Bess's hand flew up to her nose.

Nancy thought and thought. "We're going to have to figure out another way to find that marker," she said finally. "Let's try to come up with a plan by tomorrow."

But on Friday morning, when Nancy arrived in class, there was more trouble.

Mrs. Ramirez was standing next to the brooding pen. There were already a dozen or so students there, including George and Bess.

Nancy could hear the chicks peeping and chirping like crazy. They sounded upset. "What's going on?" she asked Mrs. Ramirez worriedly. "Are the chicks okay?"

"The chicks are fine," Mrs. Ramirez replied. She had a serious expression on her face. "Except for the fact that they're hungry. Their food is missing!"

ChAPTER FOUR

Where Are the Chicks?

Nancy couldn't believe it. It was bad enough that someone had destroyed Tommy's poster. How could someone steal food from a bunch of innocent little baby chicks?

The bell rang. The rest of the students poured into the room. "Hey, what's going on?" Gaby asked as she set down her backpack.

"Yeah, did someone die, or what?" Antonio said.

Mrs. Ramirez didn't reply. She turned to the entire class, looking mad. "I want to know, and I want to know right now. Who took the bag of chick food?"

No one said a word.

"If it's a joke, it's not funny. Please put the bag back right this minute," Mrs. Ramirez went on.

The class was silent.

Mrs. Ramirez shook her head. "I'm very disappointed," she said finally. "Listen up, class. I'm stepping out to ask the school secretary to go buy some more chick food. In the meantime, I want everyone to sit down in their seats and write a one-page essay about why practical jokes are a bad idea."

Tommy raised his hand. "Even me, Mrs. Ramirez?"

"Even you, Tommy," replied Mrs. Ramirez.

"Well, that's kind of unfair, since the chicks and I are the real victims here," Tommy complained.

"I'll be back in five minutes. Everyone please start writing," Mrs. Ramirez said, and left the room.

There were moans and groans all around as the students opened their notebooks. Nancy lingered by the brooding pen for a moment before taking her seat. She remembered that Mrs. Ramirez had kept the bag of chick food to the right of the brooding pen. She glanced quickly around the area. Maybe the thief had left a clue or two.

The chicks peeped and chirped noisily at Nancy. "I know you're hungry," she whispered to them. "You'll have your breakfast soon, I promise."

"This essay is dumb," Antonio said suddenly, to no one in particular.

"Shhh, we're all trying to concentrate," Gaby snapped at him.

"Someone seems to have a grudge against the poor chicks," Tommy piped up. "They're not safe here!"

"Shhh!" Gaby said again.

"They're not going to be here forever, anyway," Maya said. "I heard Mrs. Ramirez tell another teacher that when they're bigger they won't be able to stay here anymore."

"What? No one told me this! Where are they going to go?" Tommy exclaimed.

"They'll probably be sold to a restaurant and turned into fried chicken," Antonio said with a mean smile.

Several kids gasped, including Nancy, Bess, and George. "That's a terrible thing to say, Antonio!" Bess cried out.

"Well, *I'm* a vegetarian, so I don't eat chicken," Maya said.

"That's silly. *Everyone* eats chicken," said Antonio.

"Not vegetarians," Maya told him.

While the others continued talking about vegetarianism, Nancy noticed a tiny object on the floor next to the brooding pen. She picked it up.

It was a red button. Bits of red thread clung to it.

This could have fallen off the thief's clothes, Nancy thought excitedly.

She slipped the button into her pocket. As she returned to her seat, she peered around the room to see if anyone was wearing red.

But no one was—not that she could see, anyway.

"Pass the popcorn," Bess said to Nancy and George.

"Do you want caramel-flavored popcorn or pizza-flavored popcorn or regular old butter-flavored popcorn?" Nancy asked her.

"All of them, please," Bess said. The three girls giggled.

It was Friday night. Nancy, George, and Bess were having a sleepover at Nancy's house. They were sitting on Nancy's bed and chowing down on popcorn and hot chocolate that Hannah had made for them.

The girls had decided to have a mix-and-match pajama party. Nancy was wearing yellow-and-blue-striped pajama bottoms with

Hannah's red checked pajama top, which was way too big for her. George was wearing purple polka-dot pajama bottoms with a soccer jersey top. Bess was wearing a pajama top with pink hearts all over it, black leggings, and a silky pink ballet skirt.

"Okay, time to get serious," George said. "The Clue Crew has a mystery to solve."

"*Two* mysteries," Bess corrected her.

"Let's go over the clues we have so far," Nancy suggested. "We know that the marker

that was used to mess up Tommy's poster is blue-green, and it smells like bubblegum. And we have the red button I found today."

"You didn't notice anyone wearing a red outfit, though, right?" George asked her.

Nancy shook her head. "But maybe the thief stole the chick food yesterday, after school. Do you guys remember if anyone was wearing red yesterday?"

Bess closed her eyes. "Hmmm. Red outfit . . . red outfit . . . ," she chanted.

"Bess is a fashion psychic," George joked to Nancy.

Bess opened her eyes and frowned. "George, you ruined my concentration!"

Nancy took a sip of her hot chocolate. Hannah had put extra whipped cream on it, just the way she liked it. "Do you guys think the same person ruined Tommy's poster *and* stole the chick food?" she asked her friends.

"Probably," said George.

"I think definitely," Bess added.

"Do you have any ideas for suspects, Nancy?" George asked.

Nancy thought hard. "Catherine was pretty upset about the chicks' birthday on Wednesday," she said finally. "She wasn't in school today, though. Mrs. Ramirez said she sprained her ankle."

"She could have stolen the chick food yesterday, like maybe after school," Bess suggested.

"There's also Antonio," George noted. "He's a big troublemaker!"

Nancy nodded. "He's a good suspect too."

"So we have *two* suspects," said Bess. She popped a handful of popcorn into her mouth. "What do we do next? Besides eat more snacks and watch more DVDs?" She giggled.

"We should talk to Catherine and Antonio

on Monday," Nancy suggested. "And we should keep searching for more clues."

But on Monday morning, when Nancy arrived in class, things had gone from bad to worse.

Mrs. Ramirez was there. So were Principal Newman and also the janitor, Mr. Figgs. So were a bunch of students, including George and Bess.

Everyone looked really, really upset.

Nancy rushed up to her two friends. "What's going on?" she whispered. "Why are Principal Newman and Mr. Figgs here?"

"Oh, Nancy, it's awful!" Bess said. Her eyes filled with tears. "Someone stole all the baby chicks!"

ChaPTER FiVE

A Shocking Confession

Nancy was shocked. "Someone stole the chicks?" she repeated. "How? When?"

"Nobody knows," said Bess, sniffling.

"It's awful!" George cried.

Mrs. Ramirez, Principal Newman, and Mr. Figgs were deep in discussion. Everyone was listening. Nancy listened too.

"You were supposed to feed the chicks over the weekend," Mrs. Ramirez was saying to Mr. Figgs.

"I know, I know," Mr. Figgs said, nodding. "But it's like I told you. I came by on Friday after school, to check in on the wee little creatures. But they weren't here. The whole box of them was gone."

"What time was that?" Nancy spoke up.

Mr. Figgs, Principal Newman, and Mrs. Ramirez all stared at Nancy. Nancy smiled politely. She was used to grown-ups giving her funny looks whenever she was in detective mode.

"Uh, well, miss, that would have been around five o'clock," Mr. Figgs replied after a moment.

"And what time did you go home, Mrs. Ramirez?" Nancy asked her teacher.

"Around three o'clock," Mrs. Ramirez answered. "The chicks were safe and sound when I said good-bye to them," she told Principal Newman.

Principal Newman turned to Mr. Figgs. "Why didn't you let Mrs. Ramirez or me know when you came by at five o'clock and realized that the chicks were gone?"

Mr. Figgs shrugged. "I figured that maybe Mrs. Ramirez had changed her mind about having me take care of the chicks. That she'd decided to take them home for the weekend or something like that." He added, "Why, just last month, Mrs. Bailey asked me to feed the class lizard over the weekend, and she ended up taking him home and didn't tell me or even leave me a note. I figured Mrs. Ramirez did the same thing."

"Except that I didn't take the chicks home," Mrs. Ramirez said unhappily. "I wish I had. Then they wouldn't be missing!"

"Mr. Figgs, was the door locked when you came by at five o'clock?" Nancy asked him.

Mr. Figgs frowned in concentration. "I think so, yes," he said finally.

"Well, I definitely locked it when I left at three o'clock," Mrs. Ramirez declared.

Nancy thought about this. The chicks were in the classroom at three o'clock, when Mrs. Ramirez left for the day. The chicks were *not* in the classroom at five o'clock, when Mr. Figgs came by to check on them.

This meant that the chick-napper—whoever it was—had taken the chicks sometime between three and five o'clock.

Also, the chick-napper must have gotten into the locked classroom somehow. Did that mean that the person had a key?

Nancy narrowed her eyes. The Clue Crew's case had gone from one mystery to two mysteries to *three* mysteries. And the third mystery was the most serious one of all. She, George, and Bess *had* to find the poor little baby chicks.

But how?

At recess Nancy, George, and Bess were swinging on the swings and talking about the missing chicks.

"Whoever took the chicks is evil," George said.

"Really, *really* evil," agreed Bess.

Nancy pumped her legs harder so the swing would go higher. George and Bess did the same. Nearby, a group of kids was playing tag. They were shrieking and laughing loudly.

"Did the same person mess up Tommy's poster, steal the chick food, *and* chick-nap

the chicks?" Nancy wondered out loud.

"Maybe," replied George.

"I think definitely," Bess added. "Someone is out to get the poor little chicks!"

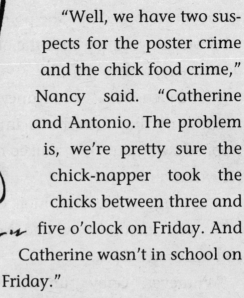

"Well, we have two suspects for the poster crime and the chick food crime," Nancy said. "Catherine and Antonio. The problem is, we're pretty sure the chick-napper took the chicks between three and five o'clock on Friday. And Catherine wasn't in school on Friday."

"She's not here today, either," Bess remarked.

"Maybe she snuck back to school on Friday just to chick-nap the chicks," George suggested.

Nancy thought about this. It was possible. But Catherine had a sprained ankle. It would not be easy to commit a chick-napping with a sprained ankle.

"Well, Antonio wasn't absent on Friday *or*

today," Bess piped up. She pointed to Antonio, who was playing tag with the other kids. "Why don't we go talk to him?"

"Good idea, Bess," said Nancy.

The girls dug their heels into the dirt and stopped swinging. They walked over to Antonio. He was arguing with Gaby.

"But I tagged you, Antonio!" Gaby insisted.

"In your dreams," replied Antonio. "You're still it, Science Geek."

"Whatever," Gaby grumbled, walking away.

Bess tapped Antonio on the shoulder. "Hi, Antonio. We need to talk to you about something."

Antonio turned around. He glanced at Bess's dress. "What do you call that color, 'Dog Vomit'?" he teased.

Bess turned bright red. She put her hands on her hips. "For your information, it's *mahogany.*"

"I like 'Dog Vomit' better," Antonio said.

Nancy put her hand on Bess's arm. "Just ignore him, he's a jerk," she whispered.

But Bess wasn't listening. She glared at Antonio. "We know you stole the baby chicks, you . . . you . . . chick-napper!" she burst out.

Antonio smiled nastily. "Okay, I confess," he said. "I did it. I stole the chicks. And I fed them to my cat Monster!"

Chapter Six

Another Detective

Nancy, George, and Bess stared at Antonio. "You did *what?*" Nancy demanded.

"Yeah, I fed the baby chicks to Monster," Antonio went on. "Monster was getting tired of Krunchies cat food."

"You are the most evil boy ever!" Bess shouted. "We're going to tell Mrs. Ramirez and Principal Newman, and you're going to go to jail for the rest of your life, and—"

Nancy watched Antonio as he listened to Bess. His dark brown eyes were gleaming mischievously.

"Bess, he's kidding," Nancy said slowly. She glared at Antonio. "That's not a very funny joke."

"Really? I thought it was hilarious. And you all fell for it!" Antonio cracked up.

"You are such a jerk," George scolded Antonio.

"So where *are* the chicks, Antonio?" demanded Bess.

Antonio shrugged. "How should I know?"

"Did you mess up Tommy's poster?" Nancy asked him.

"Did you mess up Tommy's poster?" Antonio repeated, imitating Nancy's voice. "Sure, I messed up his lame poster. Someone had to do it."

"Did you steal the chicks' bag of food?" George questioned him.

"Sure, I stole their food," Antonio said. "They really needed to go on a diet!" He laughed.

Nancy sighed. She realized that Antonio was still joking around. It was impossible to try to get a straight answer out of him. They would have to figure out another way.

"Come on," Nancy said to George and Bess. "We're wasting our time."

The three girls walked away from Antonio.

"Bye, Dog Vomit," he called out after Bess.

Bess didn't take the bait. "He is so, so evil," she said under her breath.

"He is definitely evil. I think he's hiding something too," said George.

"Hey! Clue Commandos! Excuse me!"

Nancy and her friends turned around. Gaby rushed up to them.

"Hey, Clue Commandos. You're trying to solve the mystery, right?" Gaby asked breathlessly.

"Uh, what mystery?" Nancy said innocently.

"And who are the Clue Commandos?" Bess added.

"I know you're in some sort of mystery-solving club," Gaby said to the girls. "And I know you're trying to solve the mystery of the missing chicks. I, uh, kind of overheard you talking to Antonio. Is he a suspect? What other suspects do you have?"

Nancy, George, and Bess exchanged a glance. "You . . . *overheard* us talking to Antonio?" Nancy said after a moment.

Gaby blushed. "Well, okay. I was kind of eavesdropping. But that's because I love mysteries! I love them, love them, love them! I've always wanted to be a detective. In fact, I've already started a notebook about this case. See?"

She pulled a small green notebook out of her pocket. It was covered with stickers of farm animals, like cows and horses and roosters and bunnies.

Gaby flipped the notebook open to the first page. "I don't have any clues yet. But I do have a lot of theories about the case. They're very scientific. Do you want to hear what they are?"

Before Nancy could reply, Gaby went on. "Theory Number One: Mr. Figgs the janitor stole the chicks. Motive: He really wanted a pet. I know this because I heard him telling Mrs. Ramirez once that he was thinking of getting a parakeet. Theory Number Two: Mrs. Bailey stole the chicks. Motive: She was jealous that Mrs. Ramirez had a better science project for her third-grade class than she did for her own third-grade class. Theory Number Three: The ghost of River Heights Elementary School stole the chicks—"

The bell rang then, signaling the end of recess. *Saved by the bell*, Nancy thought.

"Okay, well, thanks, Gaby," Nancy said quickly. "We'll let you know if the Clue Crew needs your help solving the case!"

"The ghost of River Heights Elementary School?" Bess said in disbelief.

"Mrs. Bailey?" added George.

"Well, at least Gaby's trying to find the chicks," Nancy said. "That's more than some people are doing."

It was after school on Monday. Nancy and her friends were walking to Catherine Spangler's house. The Spanglers lived around the corner from Nancy. Hannah had given the three girls permission to go by themselves.

The Spanglers house was white with red shutters. The front yard was filled with bright yellow daffodils that swayed in the spring breeze.

Nancy, George, and Bess went up to the front door and knocked. After a moment, a woman with honey blond hair answered the door. Nancy recognized her as Mrs. Spangler.

Then Nancy noticed something interesting. Mrs. Spangler was holding a spool of red thread, a package of sewing needles, and a small pair of scissors.

"Hello," Mrs. Spangler said with a smile. "Are you girls looking for Catherine?"

"Is she home?" Nancy asked her. "We wanted to, um, say hi and see how she was feeling."

"Well, I'm sure she'll be glad for some company," said Mrs. Spangler. "Why don't you come in and wait in the living room? I'll go find her."

"Thank you," George said.

Mrs. Spangler disappeared down the hall. "Did you guys notice the red thread and needles and scissors?" Nancy whispered to George and Bess as they sat down on the couch.

Bess nodded. "I guess Mrs. Spangler is sewing something."

"Something . . . like maybe a new red button?" Nancy suggested.

George's face lit up. "Nancy, you're a genius!"

Nancy was about to reply when she noticed something else.

She turned her head and sniffed. She sniffed again.

"Uh, Nancy? What are you doing?" Bess asked her curiously.

"Do you smell that?" Nancy asked her friends.

George and Bess began sniffing too. "It's . . . kind of sweet," said George after a moment.

"It's bubblegum!" Bess exclaimed.

Nancy glanced around the room. She spotted a sketch pad and a box of markers on a side table.

She walked over to the table and picked up

the box of markers. She sniffed and sniffed. The markers definitely smelled like bubblegum!

Nancy rooted through the markers. She had to find one that was blue-green. Or aquamarine. Or turquoise.

"What do you think you're doing, Nancy Drew?" someone demanded.

Nancy whirled around. Catherine was standing in the doorway. She looked really, really mad.

ChAPTER SEVEN

A Mysterious Box

Catherine stood in the doorway, leaning on a pair of crutches. Her right ankle was wrapped in beige-colored cloth tape.

Nancy smiled awkwardly at Catherine. George and Bess did too.

"Uh, hi, Catherine," said Nancy. She tried to think of what to say next. "I was just, uh, checking out your super-cool markers."

"No, you weren't. You were snooping," Catherine said accusingly. "My friend Payton told me you're detectives or something. Well, go find a mystery to solve somewhere else!"

Nancy was about to reply when she spotted a blue-green marker in the box of markers. She reached in and plucked it out. She tried to hide her excitement. She had found an important clue!

"Nancy, it's the aquamarine marker!" Bess blurted out.

"You mean the turquoise marker," George corrected her cousin.

Nancy held the marker out to Catherine. "This is the same color marker that someone used to mess up Tommy's poster," she said slowly. "It has the same bubblegum smell, too."

"W-what are you t-talking about?" Catherine stammered. She wobbled slightly on her crutches.

"We also found a red button near the chicks' pen, right after their food was stolen," Bess piped up.

"And speaking of red . . . we noticed that your mom is sewing something with red thread," George added.

Catherine opened her mouth, then clamped it shut.

Nancy walked up to Catherine and put a hand on her shoulder. "We know you were really upset about your birthday," she said quietly. "The chicks got lots and lots of attention. You got zero attention."

Catherine stared at Nancy for a long moment. She sighed.

"Okay, I confess," Catherine said finally. "But please don't tell my parents, okay? I'll get into such big trouble!"

"Tell us what happened," said Bess.

Catherine sighed again. "You were right . . . I mean, what you said about me being really upset about my birthday. I figured it was the chicks' fault that everyone forgot about my special day. So I . . . well, I kind of messed up Tommy's poster on Wednesday, when no one was looking. And Thursday, at the end of the day, I took the bag of chick food and hid it in the supply closet. I didn't *mean* to hurt anyone or get anyone in trouble." She hung her head and stared at the ground.

Nancy thought about this. "What about the chicks?" she asked Catherine after a moment. "Did you steal them too?"

Catherine gasped. "No way! I would never do something like that! I didn't even know about it until Payton called to tell me, like, half an hour ago." She added, "Besides, I sprained my ankle right after I came home from school on Thursday. There's no way I could have hobbled to school on my own and stolen the chicks."

Nancy thought about this, too. What Catherine said made sense. There was no way she could have committed the chick-napping with a sprained ankle.

"I'll tell Mrs. Ramirez and Tommy I'm sorry as soon as I'm back in school," Catherine went on. "I'm making Tommy a new chick poster, too. I promise." She added, "And if there's anything I can do to help you find the chicks, I'll do it! You can count on me."

"I think we should get a pizza with extra pepperoni," Nancy suggested.

"Plus green peppers and mushrooms and onions," added George.

"Plus lots and lots of pineapple." Bess giggled.

"Pineapple?" Hannah repeated with a chuckle. "I'm not sure about that one."

Nancy, George, Bess, and Hannah were sitting in a booth at Pizza Paradise. It was Monday night, and Hannah had brought the girls to the downtown pizza parlor for dinner. On the way there, the girls had filled Hannah in on the latest developments in their case, including the chick-napping.

The waitress brought a pitcher of lemonade and four glasses for the table. "I'll be back in a sec for your pizza order, ladies," she said in a friendly voice.

Hannah turned to Nancy. "So who are your suspects so far?" she asked curiously.

Nancy took a sip of her lemonade. "Well, Catherine admitted that she messed up Tommy's poster and stole the chick food."

"But she says she isn't the chick-napper, and we believe her because she sprained her ankle last Thursday," George added.

"We do have a suspect for the chick-napping," Bess piped up. "His name is Antonio. He's in our class at school. He's really, really evil."

"Why do you suspect him?" Hannah asked Bess.

"Well, because he's really, really evil, of course," Bess replied matter-of-factly. "At recess today, he told us that he'd fed the chicks to his cat, Monster. Before that, he told the whole class that the chicks would be sold to a restaurant and turned into fried chicken. Can you believe it?"

George leaned over and squinted out the window. "Hey, guys? Speaking of Antonio . . ." She pointed.

Nancy, Bess, and Hannah craned their necks. Antonio was across the street from Pizza Paradise. He was holding a cardboard box in his arms. He walked into a restaurant, carrying the box.

The sign outside the restaurant said CHEZ FANO in swirly gold letters.

"I wonder what he's doing," Nancy said, puzzled.

"And I wonder what's in that box?" added George.

Just then, Bess let out a little cry. She stood up abruptly, bumping into the table and practically spilling the entire pitcher of lemonade.

"Bess, what's wrong?" Hannah asked her, concerned.

"Antonio is walking into a *restaurant*. With a *box*," Bess practically shouted. "I bet the chicks are in that box. And I bet he's selling them to the restaurant. The chicks are going to be turned into fried chicken!"

ChaPTER EighT

A New Suspect

"No way!" Nancy and George exclaimed together.

"Way," Bess insisted.

"Antonio is evil, but he's not *that* evil," Nancy argued.

"Or is he?" George looked uncertain.

"He's the one who was talking about the chicks being turned into fried chicken," Bess reminded her friends. "Come on, guys. We have to save the poor little chicks!" She ran toward the front door.

Nancy and George followed. Hannah handed the waitress some money for the lemonades. "We're in the middle of an, um, chick emergency," she told the waitress. "We'll be back in a few minutes to order our pizzas."

"A chick emergency?" the waitress repeated, confused.

The three girls and Hannah rushed out of Pizza Paradise. They waited for a WALK signal and crossed the street.

Chez Fano was a brick building with an elegant red door. The windows had lace curtains and window boxes full of purple pansies.

"Will you go in first?" Nancy asked Hannah. "This looks like a grown-up restaurant. And you're a grown-up."

Hannah laughed. "Sure. Follow me."

Hannah opened the red door and walked in. The three girls trailed after her. "I hope it's not too late," Bess whispered to Nancy and George.

"Don't worry, Bess. If the chicks are here, we'll save them," Nancy whispered back.

Inside was a small waiting area with plush velvet chairs. Classical music played softly.

A man glanced at Nancy's group. He wore a

black tuxedo and silver wire-rimmed glasses. Nancy guessed that he must be the maître d', who was in charge of seating customers.

The maître d' pushed his glasses up his nose and frowned at Hannah. She was dressed in jeans and a gray River Heights Elementary School sweatshirt. He also frowned at the girls, who were wearing cargo pants and T-shirts.

The maître d' cleared his throat. "I am afraid that we have a dress code here at Chez Fano," he said coldly.

Bess put her hands on her hips. "Are you telling us that we don't know anything about fashion?" she demanded. "For your information, 'style' is my middle name. Do you see this T-shirt? Do you know where I got it? I got it at—"

Nancy interrupted. "Um, we're actually not here to eat dinner," she explained to the maître d'. She didn't want Bess to get into a fashion argument with him.

"Oh? Then why are you here?" the man asked.

"Does Chez Fano serve fried chicken?" George blurted out.

"Fried chicken?" the maître d' repeated. "Absolutely not. The only chicken dishes on Chez Fano's menu are . . . let us see . . . Chicken Veronique, Chicken Cordon Bleu, and Poulet Roti."

"Maybe the chicks are going to be turned into this poo-lay ro-tee or whatever," Bess whispered to Nancy and George.

Nancy turned to the maître d'. "We're looking for a boy who came in here a few minutes ago. He's eight or nine years old, tall, with dark brown hair. He was carrying a cardboard box."

The man smiled. "Ah, yes, of course. Little Tony. Are you friends of his? Why didn't you say so?"

"Little Tony?" Nancy, George, and Bess said in unison.

"Just one moment, please. I will get him for you. The maître d' disappeared through a set of double doors.

"Little Tony?" Nancy, George, and Bess said again.

A few minutes later, the maître d' returned to the lobby with Antonio. Antonio stared at the three girls and Hannah. He looked totally confused.

"W-what are you doing here?" he stammered.

"We want to know what you've done with the box of chicks," George told him.

Antonio made a face. "I don't know what you're talking about. You girls are crazy!"

Bess pointed a finger at Antonio. "You stole the chicks and brought them here! You're going to sell them to Chez Fano so they can be turned into poo-lay ro-tee!"

"We saw you walking in here with a box," Nancy added.

"A box?" Antonio said, puzzled. Then he started laughing. "Oh, *that* box. Okay, time-out here. This place is my parents' restaurant. Chez Fano. Get it? Fano is short for our last name, Elefano."

"This . . . is your parents' restaurant?" Nancy asked him, surprised.

Antonio nodded. "And that box? They're new menus. I was helping my dad carry them from our car. Wait, I'll prove it to you."

He disappeared through the double doors. He came back out, carrying the box from before.

Nancy and the girls peered into the box. It was full of . . . menus.

Nancy smiled sheepishly at Antonio. "I guess we owe you an apology."

Antonio grinned. "Yeah. Besides, I already told you. I fed the chicks to my cat Monster!"

"We're back to square one," Bess said to Nancy and George.

It was Tuesday. The girls were sitting in the cafeteria, eating lunch.

Nancy took a big bite of her peanut-butter-and-jelly sandwich. Hannah made the best peanut-butter-and-jelly sandwiches ever. "We're not *totally* back to square one," she said after a moment. "Antonio could still be our chick-napper. We just don't have any proof."

"We need to think of more suspects," George suggested. "Who else had a motive to steal the chicks?"

Nancy thought about this. Criminals had to have a motive to commit their crimes. But they also had to have the opportunity.

Catherine had a motive: She was mad at the chicks for stealing birthday attention away from her. But she didn't have the opportunity; she had a sprained ankle.

But could Catherine have gotten someone else to steal the chicks for her? Nancy wondered. Someone like her friend Payton? But that seemed like a crazy idea. Would a friend do something so *wrong* for another friend?

Nancy glanced around the cafeteria, looking for Payton. But someone—or rather, *something*—else caught her eye.

Tommy Maron—aka Mr. Chick Lover—was sitting at the next table by himself. His head was bent low over a book. He was reading it very carefully, almost like he was studying for a test.

Nancy squinted at the cover of the book. It had a picture of a chick on it. She tried to make out the title.

It was *How to Take Care of Your Pet Chicks.*

Nancy's heart began racing. Why was Tommy reading a book on chick care?

Did he steal the chicks? she wondered.

ChAPTER NiNE

Lost and Found

Nancy put down her peanut-butter-and-jelly sandwich. She leaned across the table. "Don't look now," she whispered to George and Bess. "But Tommy Maron is reading a book called *How to Take Care of Your Pet Chicks.*"

"So?" Bess whispered back. "Tommy's a chick fanatic."

Nancy nodded. "Exactly. Maybe he's such a chick fanatic that—"

"He *had* to have the chicks, even if he had to steal them," George finished. "Nancy, you're a genius!"

Bess glanced quickly at Tommy, then back at Nancy. "Omigosh! So you think that *he* might be our chick-napper?" she whispered.

"There's only one way to find out," Nancy said. She got up and walked over to Tommy's table. George and Bess followed.

"Hi, Tommy," said Nancy in a friendly voice. "What are you reading?"

Tommy looked up. "What, this?" he said, indicating his chick book.

"You stole the twelve baby chicks, didn't you, Tommy Maron?"

Nancy gasped in surprise. That question didn't come from her. Or George. Or Bess.

The person who had hurled the accusation was Gaby Small!

Gaby was marching up to Tommy's table. She had her hands on her hips, and she looked mad.

"That's why you're reading this book, isn't it, Tommy?" Gaby continued. "You're hiding the chicks in a top secret location, aren't you?"

Tommy's jaw dropped. "Um, w-what are you t-talking about, Gaby?" he stammered. "I-I didn't steal the chicks. I-I would never do anything to h-hurt them!"

Nancy stared at Gaby. She wondered if Gaby had been eavesdropping on her conversation with George and Bess—again.

Nancy turned to Tommy. "If you didn't steal the chicks, then why are you reading a book on chick care?" she asked him quietly.

"Because it's interesting," Tommy replied. "I love anything having to do with chicks. This book is full of cool facts. Did you know that some breeds of chickens lay colored eggs, like blue and green?"

"Where did you get the book?" George asked him.

"I found it on the floor near my locker this morning," Tommy explained. "I was going to turn it in to the Lost and Found right away. But then I started reading it, and I couldn't stop. I figured I'd finish reading it, *then* turn it in." He blushed. "Was that a bad thing to do? It was a bad thing to do, wasn't it?"

Nancy thought about this. "Can I see the book for a sec, Tommy?"

"Uh, sure." Tommy held out the book.

But before Nancy could take the book from Tommy, Gaby grabbed it. "I'm seizing this book as evidence," she declared, stuffing it under her arm. "You're a chick-napper, Tommy. And you're obviously covering up for your crime. I'm going to see that you're brought to justice!"

With that, Gaby turned around and marched away.

"But I didn't steal the chicks!" Tommy protested to Nancy, George, and Bess.

Nancy stared after Gaby. Gaby had told the Clue Crew the other day that she had always wanted to be a detective.

Gaby's taking this detective thing a little too far, Nancy thought.

Nancy put her books in her book bag and zipped it shut. Kids passed her in the hall, talking and laughing. It was the end of the day, and everyone was heading home.

Nancy slung her book bag over her shoulder and joined the flow of students moving toward the exit. She couldn't stop thinking about the incident at lunch with Tommy and Gaby.

Something was tugging at Nancy's brain. Was it something Tommy or Gaby had said? Or was it something Nancy had seen?

What was she missing?

As she walked, Nancy went over the case in her mind. Catherine had confessed to messing up Tommy's poster and hiding the bag of chick food. But because of her sprained ankle, she was pretty much off the hook for the chick-napping. Unless she had an accomplice, that is.

Antonio could still be the chick-napper. It was hard to get a straight story out of him, though. If they were going to pursue him as a suspect, they would have to figure out some way to make him talk.

And what about Tommy? Was he telling the truth about finding the chick-care book on the floor near his locker? Or had he chick-napped the chicks, then gone out and bought the book so he could take proper care of them?

Nancy soon reached the exit. A bunch of kids were getting onto the bus. Other kids were getting picked up by parents and babysitters. Still other kids were walking home.

Just then, Nancy spotted Gaby. She was standing next to a tall, skinny, red-haired girl who appeared to be her babysitter. The baby-sitter was wearing headphones and mouthing the words to some song. She didn't seem to be paying much attention to Gaby.

On an impulse, Nancy walked up to Gaby. "Hey, Gaby," she called out pleasantly. "I was wondering if I could see that chick-care book."

Gaby stared at Nancy. "W-what do you want with it?"

"I just want to look at it," Nancy explained. "I'll give it back. I promise."

Gaby hesitated. Then she reached into her book bag and pulled it out. "Here," she said, thrusting it into Nancy's hand. "Be careful with it, okay? It's scientific evidence in my case against Tommy Maron."

The babysitter tugged at her headphones. "Come on, Gab," she said in a bored-sounding voice. "We have to go, like, now. You have a violin lesson in fifteen minutes."

Gaby cast a worried look at the book in Nancy's hands. "Give it back to me tomorrow, okay?" she insisted. Then she turned and walked to the parking lot with her babysitter.

Nancy leaned against a tree and started flipping through *How to Take Care of Your Pet Chicks*. She studied the table of contents. She read the first few pages.

George and Bess came skipping up to her. "Ready to walk home, Nancy?" George asked her.

Bess peered at the book in Nancy's hands. "What are you reading?"

Nancy glanced up from the book. Her blue eyes were sparkling.

"I think I know who stole the chicks!" she announced.

ChaPTER TEN

A Chick Reunion

George and Nancy stared at Nancy in surprise. "You've caught the chick-napper?" George asked Nancy.

"I haven't caught the person yet. But I think I know who it is," replied Nancy.

"Who is it? Who is it?" Bess began jumping up and down with excitement.

Nancy showed the chick-care book to her friends. "Check this out and tell me what you notice," she said.

"This is Tommy's book, right?" George said.

"He told us that he found it on the floor near his locker," Nancy replied. "I think he's telling the truth."

Bess leaned over her cousin's shoulder as George began flipping through the pages. "'Your Pet Chick's New Home,'" Bess read out loud. "'What to Feed Your Pet Chick.' 'Your Pet Chick's Litter Box.'" She glanced up. "Am I missing something? I don't see any clues here."

George pointed to page three. "Hey, here's something. Someone put a cow sticker on the bottom of the page," she noted.

Bess grabbed the book from her cousin and turned more pages. "Here's a sheep sticker. And a bunny sticker. And a rooster sticker. And a horse sticker. And a piggy sticker."

"Do you remember where else we saw stickers like these?" Nancy prompted.

George scrunched up her face, thinking. Then

her eyes lit up. "Gaby's detective notebook! It was covered with farm animal stickers!"

Nancy nodded. "Exactly. I think this chick-care book is Gaby's. She lost it by accident, and Tommy found it."

Bess frowned. "So why was she acting like it was Tommy's book in the cafeteria today?"

"She wanted us to think that Tommy stole the chicks," Nancy explained. "And yesterday, she was eavesdropping on our conversation with Antonio, remember? On the playground? She was pretending to help us find the chick-napper. She had all these theories, like how the chick-napper might be Mr. Figgs or Mrs. Bailey or the ghost of River Heights Elementary School."

"Oh, yeah," George said slowly.

"I think Gaby's been trying to cover up the fact that *she's* the real chick-napper," Nancy finished.

"But why would Gaby steal the chicks?" Bess wondered. "It doesn't make any sense."

"And how did she sneak them out of Mrs. Ramirez's classroom on Friday?" George added.

"We definitely need some answers," said Nancy. "And there's only one way to get them."

It was nearly dinnertime when Hannah turned left onto a dirt road called Waddling Duck Lane. The road was lined with tall, bushy trees. The smell of honeysuckle flowers filled the air.

"I think we're almost there," Hannah called out to the girls.

Nancy, George, and Bess were sitting in the backseat. They were on their way to Gaby Small's house—or rather, the Smalls' family farm.

"What if Gaby isn't home from her violin lesson yet?" said Bess worriedly.

"What if she is, but she denies everything?" George piped up.

"We'll get her to tell us the truth somehow," Nancy said.

A few minutes later a large white farmhouse

came into view. Half a dozen chickens scattered, clucking, as Hannah's car approached. In the distance, Nancy could see a large, open field, horse paddocks, and three faded red barns.

There was a silver SUV in the driveway. "Someone's home," Nancy noted.

She, George, Bess, and Hannah walked up to the front door and knocked. The babysitter answered, still wearing her headphones. She was swaying and bopping to some song.

"Uh, hi," the babysitter said, still sounding bored. "Are you looking for Mr. and Mrs. Small? They'll be home in about an hour."

"We're actually looking for Gaby," Nancy spoke up. "Is she here?"

The babysitter gestured vaguely. "She's in one of the barns."

Nancy thanked her, and the four of them headed out back toward the barns. "Be really, really quiet," Nancy whispered to the others. "I want to surprise Gaby."

"Okay," Bess whispered back.

"I feel like a real detective," Hannah said, chuckling. "Does this mean I'm an honorary Clue Crew member?"

"Definitely," George told her.

They reached the first barn. Nancy peered through a crack in the doorway. There were animals inside, but no humans.

They went to the second barn. Again, Nancy peered inside. And again, there were animals inside, but no humans.

They went to the third barn. "She'd better be in this one," whispered Bess.

Nancy peered inside. She saw Gaby, sitting in the far corner of the barn, hovering over a cardboard box. Nancy could hear the distinctive sound of . . . peeping and chirping!

Nancy rushed into the barn, followed by George, Bess, and Hannah. "Hi, Gaby," Nancy called out. "Having fun with the chicks?"

Gaby's head shot up. She stared at Nancy and the others. "Uh . . . w-what are you d-doing here?" she stammered.

Nancy walked up to the cardboard box and peeked in. They were all there—the five yellow boy chicks and seven brown girl chicks, including Fred.

"These aren't the chicks from school," Gaby said quickly. "They're, um, *our* chicks. They came from our, um, chicken Annie Mae's eggs."

"Really?" Nancy said. "And there just happen to be five boys and seven girls? And the exact same color water dish that Mrs. Ramirez used? And the same kind of litter box? And the . . ."

"Okay, okay," Gaby said, throwing her hands up. "I admit it. I took the chicks. But it was for a really good reason!"

Bess folded her arms

across her chest. "What reason?"

"I heard Antonio say last Friday that the chicks were going to be sold to a restaurant and turned into fried chicken," Gaby said miserably. "I couldn't let that happen! I mean, you guys believed him too, right?"

Nancy, George, and Bess exchanged glances. "Uh, well, yeah, sort of," George said after a moment.

"Anyway, I had to think fast," Gaby went on. "On Friday after school, I hid in the supply closet in Mrs. Ramirez's classroom. I waited until she'd left and locked the door. Then I took the box full of chicks. I locked the door behind me. Then I snuck out the side entrance—you know, the one we're not supposed to use. No one saw me."

"Then what happened?" Nancy prompted her.

"Tiffani—that's my babysitter—was in the parking lot. I told her that Mrs. Ramirez had asked me to bring the chicks home for the weekend, to take care of them. She believed me. She believes whatever I say," Gaby explained. "When I got home, I hid them in here. We don't really use this barn anymore, so I figured my parents wouldn't find the chicks."

"What were you going to do with the chicks?" George asked her.

"I don't know. Raise them here, I guess. I didn't have a plan or anything. I just wanted to save them from becoming fried chicken!" Gaby wiped a tear from her eye.

Nancy sighed. Then she turned to George, Bess, and Hannah—and smiled.

They had found the chicks, safe and sound. The Clue Crew had solved another mystery!

"Hi, Pippy Pipsqueak!"

"Hi, Flufferina!"

"Hi, Chirping Charlie!"

"Hi, Fred!"

The kids in Mrs. Ramirez's class were gathered around the brooding pen, greeting the chicks.

Nancy, George, and Bess were right up front. The chicks were peeping and chirping excitedly. They seemed happy to be home, surrounded by so many admirers.

Gaby had returned the chicks to the school along with lots and lots of apologies. She had gotten into big trouble over the chick-napping. Mrs. Ramirez had told her that she would have to stay after school for the next four weeks. At home, Gaby's parents had taken away her television and computer privileges for a whole month.

Catherine was back in school too. Her sprained ankle was better. She, too, had apologized to both Mrs. Ramirez and Tommy. She had made Tommy a new "Welcome, Chicks!" poster. And Mrs. Ramirez told her that she would have to help clean out the chicks' cage whenever it needed cleaning.

But there was really good news too. Mrs. Ramirez had made arrangements with the Small family to take the chicks to their farm when they were old enough. There they would be able to grow up and produce more eggs—instead of fried chicken!

George turned to Nancy and Bess. "The Clue Crew does it again," she said proudly.

"We definitely cracked this case," Nancy agreed.

"Nancy, you made a joke!" said Bess. "Get it? Cracked? As in eggs?"

The three girls laughed.

Nancy, Bess, and George's
Egg Carton Garden

When it's springtime, Nancy, Bess, and George love to grow flowers, veggies, and herbs in a special container that they can make from an egg carton. You can make your own egg carton garden too!

You Will Need:
An empty egg carton with the lid cut off
Markers and stickers to decorate your
carton

Popsicle sticks to label your plants

A bag of potting soil

Packets of seeds (You might choose
easy-to-grow flowers such as sunflowers,
nasturtiums, or morning glories.
Easy-to-grow veggies and herbs include
beans, turnips, beets, and basil.)

Springtime! (After a few weeks your seeds
will have grown into little plants, called
seedlings. The seedlings will need to be
moved outside and replanted in your
yard, so this project won't work in cold
weather. If you live someplace where it's
warm year-round, then you're probably
okay no matter what season it is.)

To Make Your Container:

❀ Using a sharp pen or pencil, poke a little hole
in the bottom of each egg cup. This way, when
you water your plants, the extra water will be
able to run out the bottom. Your plants like wet
soil, not super-soggy soil!

❀ Decorate the outside of the cups with markers and stickers. Think of fun spring designs using flowers, butterflies, chicks, and bunnies. Or come up with a unique design that's all your own!

❀ Fill each cup with potting soil—somewhere between halfway and totally full, so there's a little room at the top. Pat each cupful of soil with your fingers so it's packed firm but not rock hard. Set aside the remaining bag of potting soil for later, when you plant the seeds.

To Make Your Labels:

❀ You might want to plant the same kind of seed in all twelve egg cups. Or you might want to plant different kinds of seeds: maybe six of one kind and six of another; or four, four, and four. Make labels for each kind of seed by writing the name of the plant on a clean Popsicle stick. You can use a marker, pen, or pencil.

❀ If you don't want to use Popsicle sticks, you can also write the name of the plants directly on the egg cups.

Now You're Ready to Plant!

❀ With your finger, poke each cupful of potting soil in the middle so you get a little hole about one inch deep.

❀ Place a seed or two in each hole. If it's a big seed, just use one. If they're itty-bitty seeds, you can sprinkle a few into each hole. Use more potting soil to fill in the hole. With your finger, gently pat and press the top of the soil. (Important: Make sure to keep the seed packets, even if they're empty; you'll need the directions on them for later on, when you replant the seedlings outside.)

❀ Keep track of which seed is in which hole with your Popsicle stick labels. Place each label in the dirt, near the edge of the cup. Don't stick the label in the middle of the cup, right where you put the seeds.

❀ After you're done planting, water each cup. The soil should be moist (like the ground after a light rain), not flooded (like the ground after a huge storm). It's always best to water slowly and gradually, until it seems just right; you can always add more if you need it.

❀ Put your egg container garden in a sunny window, on a towel or other surface that your parents won't mind getting a bit wet or dirty. If one window in your house gets lots of morning sun, and another window in your house gets lots of afternoon sun, you might move your egg carton garden from one window to the other every day.

Watch Your Plants Grow!

❀ Over the next few days and weeks, your seeds will grow into seedlings. Have fun watching them poke out of the top of the soil, then slowly get taller and taller.

❀ Check the soil with your finger every day. If it feels dry, add more water.

❀ Once the seedlings become too tall for their egg cups, you will need to move them outside. Ask your parents to check the weather reports to make sure it's warm enough to do this. In general, temperatures should be well above freezing every night before you move your seedlings outside.

❀ When you're ready to move your seedlings outside, find a sunny spot in your yard. Dig twelve holes in the ground with a small spoon from your kitchen; the holes should be about four inches apart from one another and two or three inches deep. (You can ask your parents for help.) Use the same spoon to dig out the seedlings, including the soil, from each of the egg cups. Be very careful not to hurt the roots. Place each seedling (and soil clump) in its own hole. The roots should fit in the hole *below* ground level; the rest of the seedling should be *above* ground level. Fill in the holes with more soil and pat gently. Water.

❀ If you don't have a yard, you could use a big pot or several big pots. You could also find out if there is a community garden in your neighborhood and plant your seedlings there.

❀ Make sure to check on your seedlings every day and water regularly, especially when there hasn't been any rain.